Happy
Reader

PAGES *of* MUSIC

G. P. Putnam's Sons
New York

PAGES of MUSIC

by Tony Johnston

pictures by Tomie dePaola

For Tomie dePaola,
an artist who "makes paint sing."
                        —T J

Text copyright © 1988 by Tony Johnston.
Illustrations copyright © 1988 by Tomie dePaola.
All rights reserved. Published simultaneously in Canada.
Printed in Hong Kong by South China Printing Company.
Book design by Nanette Stevenson.

Library of Congress Cataloging-in-Publication Data
Johnston, Tony.   Pages of music.
Summary: A childhood visit to Sardinia
haunts a composer, who returns there one
Christmas to repay with his music the
kindness of the island's inhabitants.
[1. Music—Fiction.   2. Christmas—Fiction.
3. Sardinia—Fiction] I. De Paola,
Tomie, ill.   II. Title.
PZ7.J6478Pag   1988   [E]   87-6928
ISBN 0-399-21436-4

First impression.

Long ago a painter and her son, Paolo, visited the island of Sardinia. The mother had heard how beautiful it was in spring, and she wanted to paint it then.

It was an island of mountains leaning over bays, hills sprinkled with wild flowers and sheep, and everywhere the sound of shepherds' pipes.

Beautiful as it was, it was also a poor island. The people were poor because the land was poor. They scratched it with sticks, and dug it with hoes, and turned it over with the help of oxen. Still, they were able to grow only enough grain and olives to live from day to day.

The mother bought olives and cheese in a village, and they went into the hills, where she could paint and Paolo could play.

One day a shepherd saw her painting his flock. He could tell from the picture that she loved the island.

"You must be tired from painting so many sheep," he said. "Come. Eat something with me."

"We have olives," said the mother.

"We have cheese," said Paolo.

"But you need more," the shepherd said. "You need *fogli di musica*, pages of music."

Paolo loved music. At home he practiced his music very hard. But he could not eat it.

"What is *that*?" he asked excitedly.

"You will see."

They went to the shepherd's hut, sat on wooden stools,
and shared his *fogli di musica*, which was a thin, hard bread.

When they had finished, the mother offered to pay the shepherd. But he just smiled, took up his pipe, and filled the air with sweet notes.

Paolo began to dance and sing with such joy that the shepherd leaped up and danced too. The mother sailed her hat into the wind and laughed.

So it was throughout Sardinia. Paolo and his mother wandered the hills. She painted the sheep, the shepherds, the beautiful land. Wherever they went, shepherds shared what little they had with them, their *fogli di musica*. And Paolo listened to the music of their pipes. And he loved it.

At last they went home. As they traveled to the main-
land, Paolo looked at the island far away.
"One day I will go back there," he said.

Years passed and Paolo grew up. He studied music. He played music. He wrote compositions. And he became a famous composer. People heard his music in the concert halls of Europe.

"He writes like an angel," they said. And he did.

Paolo wrote for organs. For harps. For whole orchestras. But in his heart he still heard shepherds' pipes. To him they made the most beautiful sound of all.

He wanted to write music for them. So he did.

He worked and worked on the music. As he worked, he remembered the shepherds who had shared their bread with him and his mother. He remembered what he had said, *One day I will go back there.* Then he had a wonderful idea. And he smiled.

One Christmas morning something incredible happened in a village in Sardinia.

It was so early, the sun had not yet risen. The villagers heard something. Creaking.

"Birds do not creak," they said. "But what else is awake at this hour but birds?"

They poked their heads out of windows and doors. The creaking got louder.

"Cos'è questo?" they asked. "What is this?"

Far away, a procession of wagons was crawling over their hills. As it got closer, the villagers saw that the wagons were full of men and women grandly dressed in black and white.

"Cos'è questo?" they asked.

The wagons stopped in front of the church. A man jumped down and began directing things. He moved so quickly that his hair bounced and his bow tie jiggled. He seemed to be everywhere at once. It was Paolo.

"Quick, quick, quick," he said. "Everybody out. Careful with the instruments. That's it. Very fine. Yes, please. Gently, gently, *gently*."

Like so many eggs, the percussions and woodwinds and strings were set down on the street, then carried inside the church. Gently, gently, *gently*.

And before anyone could say *santo piccolo*, an entire symphony orchestra was settled comfortably there.

Then Paolo told everyone, "When the shepherds come, the music will begin."

The musicians spent the day laughing, eating, and sharing stories with the people while they waited for the shepherds to come to the church, as they would, for it was Christmas.

At last the shepherds came down from the hills. As they neared the church, they heard something. Creaking.

"Crickets do not creak," they said. "But what else could that be at this hour but crickets?"

They poked their heads through the church doors.

"*Cos'è questo?*" they asked.

It was Paolo's orchestra getting settled.

"I am Paolo," Paolo said. "I am grown up. Do you remember?"

And they did.

"Once you shared your *fogli di musica* with me," he told them. "Now I will share mine with you."

Flutes began to play a simple shepherds' song. Violins joined in. And the organ. And horns. Until at last the whole orchestra was playing.

It was a song of a night long ago, a blazing star, and shepherds come to meet a child.

As the notes swelled up, a joyful feeling filled the church. For everyone felt the beauty of the song and the warmth of Christmas, sharing Paolo's *fogli di musica.*